HOW WE WERE

HOW WE WERE

FOUR STORIES BY

TEDDY JAM

WITH PICTURES BY

Ange Zhang

GROUNDWOOD BOOKS | HOUSE OF ANANSI PRESS
TORONTO   BERKELEY

Groundwood Books / House of Anansi Press
110 Spadina Avenue, Suite 801, Toronto, Ontario M5V 2K4
or c/o Publishers Group West
1700 Fourth Street, Berkeley, CA 94710

We acknowledge for their financial support of our publishing program the Canada Council for the Arts, the Government of Canada through the Book Publishing Industry Development Program (BPIDP) and the Ontario Arts Council.

 ONTARIO ARTS COUNCIL
CONSEIL DES ARTS DE L'ONTARIO

Library and Archives Canada Cataloguing in Publication
Jam, Teddy
How we were / Teddy Jam, author ; Ange Zhang, illustrator.
Contents: The year of fire – The stoneboat – The kid line – The fishing summer
ISBN-13: 978-0-88899-901-6 (bound)
ISBN-10: 0-88899-901-1 (bound)
I. Zhang, Ange II. Jam, Teddy. Year of fire. III. Jam, Teddy. Stoneboat. IV. Jam, Teddy. Fishing summer. V. Jam, Teddy. Kid line. VI. Title.
PS8569.A427H69 2008   jC813'.54   C2008-902511-3

Design by Michael Solomon
Printed and bound in China

CONTENTS

*

THE YEAR OF FIRE

1 IN MARCH my mother drives me out from the city to help my grandfather make maple syrup.

His house backs into a hill so the wind can't make it cold. And on top of the hill, the maples start. Near the house just a few are left, big lonely trees with long branches that stick into the winter sky. But if you follow the hill past the barn and the pasture, there is suddenly a whole little forest of maples with a stone firepit at the bottom of the hill.

At maple syrup time my mother leaves me at my grandfather's house. His brother John comes out from town to cook for me and my grandfather while we make syrup in the old forest.

My grandfather sits in front of the boiling pan, feeding the fire. My job is to bring wood when my grandfather asks, help empty the buckets from the trees, and listen to my grandfather's stories.

Under the pan is a big fire, the biggest fire I've ever seen. One day, kneeling down and looking into it so close my face felt like it was burning, I asked my grandfather if he had ever seen a bigger fire than this.

"A bigger fire than this?" my grandfather repeated. He pushed back his hat and scratched his head. "I could tell you about a fire so big you wouldn't believe it."

"I would," I promised. My grandfather Howard always makes me promise to believe his stories.

"Okay," he said, the way he always does. "I'll tell you about a fire, the biggest I ever saw, the biggest there ever was around here."

He closed his eyes. My grandfather likes to close his eyes when he tells a story. Once I asked him why and he told me that when he closes his eyes he can see himself when he was a little boy.

2 "When this fire happened, this big fire, I was your age. I had just started my third year at Mrs. Brown's schoolhouse. John was a year ahead. It was fall, and one night after supper I was going to the woodshed with my father to get some kindling for the stove. It was the middle of October. There was no

snow but the ground was frozen hard. The cattle and the horses were already in their barns. I used to like standing outside listening to them eat. Did you ever hear a whole barnful of animals chewing at once? I stopped to listen to them that night. And then after a little while I began to smell smoke. It was a thick heavy smell and when I turned my face to the wind it made me cough.

"My father was running up the hill. I ran after him. The smoke was coming from the Richardson swamp fields, back of the village. We couldn't see any flames but there was light in the sky. There's a house there now, but back then those fields were only half cleared. They'd been working on them that fall, cutting down the trees, dragging the logs to the creek, and stacking the brush in the middle of the field.

"My father always blamed Richardson for the fire, though he never said so exactly, just shook his head. But that night, standing on the hill, he said, 'Richardson must have been burning brush this afternoon. Now the wind's gone up.'

"Later on Mr. Richardson said he would never have burned brush at that time of year. That was 1919, the year after the First World War ended, and sometimes returned soldiers came through, just wandering the countryside and hiring themselves out for chores. Richardson said he'd seen two men with packs earlier that day, and that they must have started a campfire, using the brush for shelter.

"We went back into the house, your great-grandfather and I. Nowadays a person would just pick up the telephone, but there was none then. My father had the next best thing, a fast horse he used to ride around the township. My mother never liked him riding at night, said he'd fall off and break his neck somewhere and die in the dark. Whenever she said that my father would just rub his hands together and start looking for his hat.

"The night of the fire was so cold you could hear the horse-shoes ringing on the frozen road as my father galloped up toward the village. I sat at the kitchen table, trying to color a map for geography class.

"John was probably whittling. I never saw such a man for carving wood. Do you know he made all those puppets in the kitchen? He used to give your mother a puppet every Christmas."

My grandfather Howard looked into the fire. Sometimes his stories turned into each other, like a long braided rope connecting him to when he was a boy.

"I wanted to see the fire," my grandfather said. "I was doing my homework but I was wishing I could be out there in the middle of things.

"We had thought my father would be right back, but after an hour had passed my mother and I and John went outside. Now you could smell the smoke right from the porch. We went running past the barns and up the hill to look.

"Back of Richardson's swamp was a section of government land, all in oak and elm trees with a bit of cedar. Everyone used to call it the forest. Some of the trees were so big around you could hide behind one on a horse. The forest was split by the creek they used to use for floating logs down to the lake.

"The fire was growing before our eyes, a wall of flame shooting up into the sky, trees exploding in great showers of sparks, so loud you could hear them right across the valley. The air was filled with birds, too, crying and cawing and cheeping like it was the end of the world."

3 "We were on our way back to the house when we heard my father riding down the road. He galloped right by us to the shed, pulled open the door, and started dragging out the cart. My mother ran to the kitchen and began throwing buckets out the door. At the time we were all scared, but later, when we'd sit around talking about the fire, everyone always started to laugh at the memory of my mother standing at the kitchen door, throwing metal pails at us. They came sailing out the door one by one, then bounced clanging down the frozen grass.

"While my father hitched up the horse, I threw the buckets and some shovels and axes into the cart. Then John and I jumped in after them. My father didn't notice us until we were halfway down the road. And then, instead of sending us back, he just said: 'Do what I tell you.'

"At the creek all the men were cutting down trees and trying to make a space wide enough that the fire couldn't jump across. The fire was burning so loud everyone had to shout. John and I were supposed to fill the buckets in the creek and carry them to the men.

"By now, the fire took up the whole sky. All the boys were there helping their fathers. John was already so strong he could carry two buckets to my one. Bits of wood started to fly through the air like bombs, closer and closer. Everyone soaked themselves in the creek so they wouldn't catch on fire, then they kept work-ing – until a giant branch landed in the creek with a big hiss, like a burning crocodile, and exploded all over everyone.

"John was the one standing closest to it. He gave the loudest yell you ever heard and we all splashed through the water toward him.

He had his hands over his face. When my father took them away we saw John's eyebrows had been burned right off his forehead.

"More fiery branches started landing in the creek. Everyone decided to go home and try to save their houses.

"That night the whole forest burned down, also Richardson's field and every tree on both sides of the creek. The next day the fire was still burning. Everywhere you went the trees were in flames. The entire province might have burned down if it hadn't started to rain. Not a little rain either. One of those big heavy October rains that knocks every last leaf off the trees and keeps going until you look outside and there's nothing left of summer.

"Richardson lost his house. We were all right – that was because there were so few trees near our house or barn. One year my father's father had broken his leg and couldn't take the team back into the woods to cut firewood. When winter came he just

limped out from the house, cutting whatever he could get to in order to stay warm.

"The next day after the fire my mother took us and the Richardson kids to my aunt's house in town. Then she came back to help my father. The schoolhouse burned down, too. They didn't build another one until the next summer. You would have thought we'd have a whole year's holiday, but instead of that Mrs. Brown taught us our lessons in the church all winter.

"After a couple of days a crew from the army came to finish fighting the fire. By then the rain had slowed it down and, anyway, there were hardly any trees left standing. You could walk along the road or go up to the ridge behind the house, and instead of seeing woods, all of a sudden there was nothing but blackened tree trunks and burned grass, all of it still smoking. You might have thought the world had come to an end. It looked so awful you kept turning your head away.

"Two weeks later it started to snow. I was never so glad to see it. The snow piled up so high that by New Year's Day I even began to forget what was under it."

4 My grandfather stopped talking. He picked up a long stick and poked at the fire. I looked at the flames as they shot up around the syrup pan. But my face got hot, so I pulled away.

While my grandfather got some more logs, I opened the knapsack and took out the lunch John had made us. It was peanut butter sandwiches and carrots. I pushed some snow off a log and lined up our sandwiches. Then I heard a loud noise and looked up. A blue jay was sitting on the bare branch of one of the maple trees my grandfather had tapped. Its feathers made me think of my great-uncle John's eyebrows in the fire. They were gray and bristly now, with big tufts of black hair that stuck out at the sides.

"Did he have to go to the hospital?"

"Who?"

"John."

"I'll tell you what happened. Mother put butter over the burns. Every single morning for months. John's eyebrow hairs got to look like porcupine quills sticking through the grease."

When we had finished our lunch my grandfather led me along the ridge at the top of the hill. There was a big slab of rock where the sun had melted a space to sit.

At the far end of the rock was a stump. It was a strange stump because you could see its roots, and they were buried in the creases of the rock. My grandfather saw me looking at the stump, then handed me his hunting knife. It was big and its handle was bumpy, like my grandfather's hand. The handle was an old yellow piece of bone but the blade was sharp and shiny.

"Take a piece of that root," my grandfather said.

I broke a piece off, whittled at it with my grandfather's knife. Some of it was just waiting to fall apart and crumbled into dark gray dust. When I got down to the core of the root, little yellow-red splinters came off like tooth-picks.

"Cedar," my grandfather said. "Richardson's swamp was filled with cedar and everyone in the country had it on their land. Used it to make fences and kin-dling. When spring came that year, there was still a lot of cedar standing, but all the needles were gone. Then, when the snow melted, the trunks started to fall over. The fire had been smolder-ing underground all winter beneath the snow, eating away the roots, so that as soon as the deep snow melted, there was noth-ing left to hold up the trees. They just fell over. By the time all the snow was gone the ground was covered by ten thousand trees, lying on their sides."

I closed my eyes. Ten thousand trees. I wondered if anyone had heard them falling. I wondered what kind of noise they had made plopping into the soft snow and mud, and if they all fell at once or one at a time, like leaves in October.

"During Easter vacation we came back here with the horses and loaded the wagons with all the wood that was still good for burning. There was some cedar still standing. Those trees had been so deep-rooted that, even though the fire kept on burning under the snow, those roots held onto the only secure thing down there, the rocks.

"You see that?" My grandfather pointed to the ragged edge at the top of the stump. "I sawed that tree, right there. Used my father's bucksaw. It was the first tree I ever cut."

The blue jay had followed us from the maple grove. My grandfather reached into his pocket and threw it a crust.

"When spring came that year, the grass was greener than ever. All that black burned ground sprouted grass the way it never had before. Then after a few years the trees started growing again, so you could stand at the top of the hill and you'd see green leaves again in the valley, just the way you used to except they were brighter and didn't stick up quite so high in the sky. Now, if it weren't for these stumps, you might never know the fire had even happened."

5 We went back down to our fire. My grandfather reached into his pocket and pulled out a plastic bag with some cookies.

"What's the end of the story?" I asked him.

"The end of the story?" My grandfather looked up at the big maple trees pushing into the sun.

"First the fire burned. Then the spring came and the grass was green. Finally, after a very long time, the trees grew back. Pretty soon no one knew about the fire except for a few grand-fathers. But no one asked them about it. Then there was only one grandfather who remembered it, and even he was starting to forget. Until one day when he was looking at some burning wood and a girl asked him about the biggest fire he ever saw. So he told the girl about the biggest fire he ever saw. One day there won't be anyone who remembers the fire, only people who remember the story. So you're at the end of the story. Unless you tell it to someone else."

He reached into the plastic bag, took out one of the cookies and bit into it. "Don't forget to tell them about John's eyebrows. While his face was getting better he had to stay at home for two weeks. When he got bored my mother taught him how to make cookies, just like these."

Which was how the story ended, until I made my grandfather tell it to me again.

THE STONEBOAT

THE SPRING, when the melting snow makes Lion's Creek roar, is the time to go looking for catfish.

One Saturday after milking, my brother Evan and I went down with some fishing lines and a couple of buckets.

It was early morning. There were still patches of snow on the hills and the rising sun sent out a pink light that made those snow patches glow like wrapping paper.

Evan stood at the edge of the water wearing Dad's big boots, looking for fish to scoop up with his bucket.

I sat on the bank with my line. I used bread and a piece of bacon for bait.

After about fifteen minutes, when I hadn't caught anything, I walked up the creek a bit, around a corner where the water turned white as it foamed up the side of a big rock.

That was when I saw Mr. Richard, as my father called him. I found out later his name used to be pronounced Ree-shard, because sometime back before anyone but the schoolteacher's mother could remember, his family had been French. Back then,

Mr. Richard's grandmother had been called Madame Ree-shard, and she would come to the school to teach French twice a week.

Mr. Richard was standing in the water like a big black-bearded statue wearing hip boots. He had a stained old fedora on his head, and a pitchfork in each hand poised above the roiling white water.

The sound of Lion's Creek was louder than a shout, so I said, "Hello, Mr. Ree-shard," because I knew he wouldn't hear me.

There was no place for me to put my line. The water was moving too fast. Just as I was about to turn back, I saw Mr. Richard stab one of his pitchforks down into the water. A second later it came up, a big silvery catfish writhing on its tines. He threw it onto the bank of the creek, then stabbed again. Over and over the big pitchforks slashed into the water. Again and again catfish were thrown wriggling onto the bank.

That spring Lion's Creek was huge. The water rushed through with a deafening roar, whirling and dancing as it smashed past rocks and logs. Sheets of icy spray were thrown up onto the bank where I stood watching Mr. Richard.

His beard was dripping and his mouth looked grim and sour. With each stab he stepped forward to meet the force of the water.

Suddenly he raised both pitchforks at once. With his black beard, his filthy hat, his giant arms spread out to kill, he looked like a vengeful horrible god preparing for a sacrifice.

Then he lost his footing and fell into the water.

His hat was swept away, and I could see his bare head, black hair plastered back from his white forehead. His head looked like a ball, a ball bouncing on the surface of the fast-moving water as he struggled to regain his balance.

"Evan," I screamed.

I saw Mr. Richard's head bounce against one of the rocks. Blood gushed out of the wound, and suddenly the white water was streaked with pink.

I was trying to get to him in the water, but I could only come close enough to stick my fishing rod out toward his hand. He pushed it away and instead held out a pitchfork, handle first. I grabbed hold of it and was trying to use it to pull him up when I felt Evan's arms around my waist.

"Hang on or I'll kill you," Evan said. Then he yanked me back so hard that I thought my arms would come off.

"You know what?" my sister said that night. "You should have let Mr. Richard drown. We'd be a lot better off because Dad owes him two hundred dollars and doesn't know how he's ever going to pay it."

She was in the bedroom I shared with Evan. We hadn't told our parents what had happened at Lion's Creek. We were afraid that if we did, we wouldn't be allowed to go fishing.

"Two hundred dollars," I repeated. For only five hundred dollars the bank had made the Longleys sell their farm down the road. Evan and I went to the auction but left partway through. Afterwards the Longleys, on their way to live out west with Mrs. Longley's brother, brought us their cats.

Now I suddenly felt confused and sick to my stomach. Then I had an idea. "Well, he must think his own life is worth two hundred dollars," I said. "I saved it for him. He can't make Dad pay now."

But of course he could. Mr. Richard was his own law. He had the best land in the township and was famous for working it eighteen hours a day. He made more money than anyone else, then loaned it when others ran out of cash. Sometimes he could be seen standing in the parking lot at the church, collecting the weekly instalments everyone owed him in a big dark sock that bulged in his pocket all during service.

A week later, one Friday night when my parents had gone to a neighbor's for dinner, I snuck out after I was supposed to be in bed and walked past the barn toward the Richards' land.

I knew he'd be out there. Spring nights were perfect for removing the rocks that had heaved up into the fields during the winter. They would snag the plow if they weren't taken out before spring planting.

It wasn't so late. There was almost a full moon. It was halfway up the sky, shining so brightly that the trees made shadows. From far away I could hear the clinking of Mr. Richard's shovel and

crowbar against the fieldstones. As I drew closer I could hear him grunting as he pulled out the rocks and threw them into the stoneboat, where they thudded into the wood bottom.

"I know my father owes you two hundred dollars," I was going to say to him. "But Evan and I saved your life..." That was as far as I had it worked out. I couldn't offer to work for him in the summer because my father needed us on our own farm. Maybe he would just see that my father was drowning in debt the way he had been drowning in the creek. Maybe he would reach in to help my father the way we had helped him. Or maybe he would just push his hat down on his head and pretend he hadn't heard me.

Even as I went up to him, Mr. Richard kept on working. With a long iron bar even taller than he was, he was trying to pry a huge boulder out of the ground.

When he had one edge free, I pushed the shovel underneath so it would stay raised. For a while we kept working around the boulder without talking. Each time he levered it higher, I would put a bar or a rock beneath. Finally it was raised enough that he could roll it away from its bed and onto the field.

There it lay, a giant pale egg in the moonlight, big enough to fill the crib my sister used to sleep in when she was a baby.

We stood beside it, panting and sweating. Mr. Richard had his sleeves rolled up. His arms were huge, even bigger than my father's. Down one was a long raised scar. Ever since I was little I'd known the story of how his house had burned down when he was a child, and his mother and two sisters had been killed.

I tried to gather my breath and my courage, finally ready to say my piece.

Mr. Richard pulled a pipe from his pocket. He sat down on

the rock and began to stuff the pipe with tobacco. I sat down on the stoneboat.

Mr. Richard reached into his overalls again and pulled something out, tossed it toward me.

It was a large apple, getting soft the way spring apples do, but it would be my first apple in a month. I slowly wiped it clean on my shirt, then took a bite. Suddenly I remembered the Bible story about Adam taking a bite from the forbidden apple, and I had the terrible feeling that Mr. Richard had somehow tricked me.

"Thanks," he said. "You're a strong boy."

After we'd pulled him out of the river, Mr. Richard had sat on the bank for a long time, coughing water and trying to get his breath. The cut had stopped bleeding and he'd pulled his hat down to cover it. Then he'd stood up, gone behind a tree, brought up all the water that was still in his stomach and lungs.

"You boys go home now," he'd said. That was all.

Now he had taken off his hat and was sucking hard on his pipe. The burning tobacco glowed like a giant coal in the darkness, sending streaks of light up onto his face. I could see a big bandage wrapped around his head.

"When I finish this apple I'm going to talk," I said to myself. But as I got down to the core, Mr. Richard seemed so huge in the moonlight that every time I opened my mouth, it closed all by itself.

I put the core in my pocket, not sure Mr. Richard would like me throwing it into the field, the way I would have done at home. Maybe he saved his apple cores for his pigs, or took out all the seeds and tried to grow trees from them.

"I'll put this rock in," Mr. Richard said. "Then we'll dump everything on the fence."

He stood up from the rock, turned to face it, arched his back, then knelt before it like a weightlifter. He stretched out his arms, put one hand under either end, then with a grunt stood up, staggered forward a step, dumped the huge boulder into the stoneboat.

Mr. Richard was wiping his hands on his overalls when I saw

my father crossing the field toward us. He was walking in a certain way I recognized, his arms swinging with each step. He must have come home and discovered my room empty.

"Strong boy," Mr. Richard said. "Knows how to lend a hand."

My father was on the other side of the stoneboat. He was surveying the load, the distance from the fence. It occurred to me my father might have come without even knowing I was there. Maybe he wanted to borrow more money. Or get more time to pay the other loan back.

Mr. Richard looked back and forth between us, as though he was curious to see what would happen. Then he stepped in front of the stoneboat, strapped himself into the leather harness and leaned into the weight.

The stoneboat had two long skids, like a sled. Once going, it would slide over the slick grass. But now Mr. Richard was bent almost down to the ground, huffing and panting as though he might explode.

I went to the back of the stoneboat to push. "Here it comes," my father said, joining me and lifting so hard that the skids of the stoneboat were freed from their ruts. With another grunt, Mr. Richard lurched forward and the boat began its slow creep across the field.

When we got to the fence, Mr. Richard unstrapped himself, then wiped the back of his hand across his mouth, as though he had just finished a meal.

The three of us positioned ourselves at the side of the boat. Later on my father said there must have been a ton of rocks, though of course that wouldn't have been possible.

The two men were sour with sweat. I was so tired from lifting and pushing I thought I must have hurt myself. Then I saw that Mr. Richard's cut had started bleeding again. The whole side of his face was covered with blood. He raised his hand and pushed at it, as though it were some kind of bug that would just fly away. I was too frightened to say anything.

"Now we push it over," he said, and without waiting for us he leaned into the stoneboat. I pushed as hard as I could while Mr. Richard and my father groaned and strained. Then suddenly Mr. Richard made a funny sound in his throat and the entire stoneboat rose in the air, almost fell back, then toppled upside down over the fence.

My father turned to me, "Guess you'd better go home now," he said.

I stood waiting for Mr. Richard to explain that in fact I was working for him, or had saved his life, or anything at all. But he just looked at me, as did my father. After a while I started walking. I was halfway across the field when I heard Mr. Richard say, "Thank you, neighbor."

When I got home, my mother was sitting on the front porch.

If she knew where I had been, she didn't say. When my father arrived he kissed me, then lifted me up on his shoulder and carried me up to bed the way he used to when I was little.

"Everything is settled," was all he told me.

Years later Mr. Richard sold his farm and bought a small house on Lion's Creek, where it widens into a small lake. Once when I was at home for a visit I discovered that my father had become friends with him, and that they often went fishing together summer mornings.

THE KID LINE

WHEN HE WAS YOUNG, my father worked on building Maple Leaf Gardens. "Right there," he'd say. "Look at that brick. I laid that brick. I remember." We'd be standing across the street when he pointed out his bricks, the ones he said he remembered.

Sometimes it would be winter, so dark and so cold that my feet were already frozen and I would be wanting to go home. Or it could be later in the year. March or April if the Leafs were in the playoffs.

December and April were my favorite months for hockey. December because I liked playing shinny in the park while the sky lost its blue, as though someone had just poured it out. Then the lights would come on and I'd be skating as fast as I could down the rink, and with every cut of my blades against the ice I'd be thinking, Look out, Big Train.

Big Train was my father's favorite player. Big Train Lionel Conacher and his brother Charlie who played for the Leafs.

The Conacher brothers, when they were boys, went to Jesse Ketchum Public School. So did my father after them. He played hockey and football with them and talked about how it was to have gotten run over by Big Train when he was only nine years old and about how getting run over by Big Train was like getting driven over by a cement truck even then, or so my father said.

After the Conacher brothers finished at Jesse Ketchum they became professional athletes, and my father could read their names in the papers. After my father finished school he started as an apprentice to a bricklayer, like his father, and he worked on Maple Leaf Gardens, which is where Charlie Conacher became a big star and led the league in scoring two times.

While Charlie Conacher was getting famous, my father built more buildings. After that he went to the war and he came back. My mother used to say the war had knocked my father off his tracks. Like he'd gotten hit by a Big Train, I used to think.

By the time I got old enough to know what my father did, what he did was sell tickets outside Maple Leaf Gardens on game night. I would go with him.

Other people who sold tickets would walk up and down outside the arena yelling out their seat location and prices. They'd be wearing bright team windbreakers and sometimes wearing toques.

Not my father. "You look like a doctor," my mother would say. She was the family expert on fashion. She worked at the Eaton's store on College Street kitty-corner from the Gardens. Sometimes my father would meet her there for lunch, on his way to buy tickets for that night. He had a long wool coat and a movie star kind of hat that he'd pull down over his forehead as though he didn't want to be recognized. He had his corner where

he always stood, away from the hustle, and sometimes in the very coldest weather he would drink coffee out of a thermos, coffee so thick with milk and sugar that I was also allowed a few gulps to warm up.

Halfway through the game we'd go home and listen to the rest of the game on the radio. Often a sports announcer or someone

writing in the paper would say something about the Conacher brothers. Of course their playing days were over. Big Train had run for Parliament and Charlie had coached for a while. "Used to play with them," my father would say. He had a dreamy way of talking as though he'd decided his whole life was a dream.

One day we were skating, whirling around the rink, my father wearing his long overcoat the way he always did.

"I bet I can beat you," I said, and we raced around the rink, my father always a few strides behind as I beat him to the line I'd scratched across the ice. And then, as I was trying to catch my breath, my father made a little circle, taking off his coat so that he was just wearing the blue sweater he always brought skating, and suddenly he was off again, his arms swinging from side to side as he picked up speed until finally he was going so fast that I started to cry because I was afraid he wouldn't be able to stop.

One night I was standing a few steps away from my father while he was selling the last of his tickets. The game had already started and soon it would be time to go home. "Reds," I heard my father say. Reds were the best seats. "I haven't had any Reds for two hours. Nothing left but a few Greens." I looked up. My father was talking to a big man, unshaven. Sometimes, those very occasional times when my father had unsold tickets, we'd go and watch the game ourselves.

I couldn't hear what the man was offering my father, but I could see my father shrugging, as though he'd decided he'd rather use the tickets than sell them for so little. Then suddenly my father came up to me and said we were going inside, too, the three of us.

It was a March night. The Leafs were playing the Bruins and fighting for a playoff spot. By the time we got in, the Leafs were already down 2-1.

In those years Ted Kennedy was the Leafs' best player. Famous for his intensity, he had already helped the Maple Leafs win a Stanley Cup as part of the New Kid Line. The Old Kid Line, the first, had of course starred Charlie Conacher.

I was sitting between my father and the stranger. When the Bruins scored their third goal, the stranger gave a little grunt. One of his hands took hold of the seat in front of us, and I saw that his knuckles were huge and swollen, the way hockey players' knuckles get, my father had explained to me, either from fighting or getting hit with the puck.

Then I saw that the man had a big scar along one cheek, and another line that might have been a scar on his chin. I should have recognized him right away. Charlie Conacher. His picture was up in the hall of our school, and my father had shown me his Conacher brothers scrapbook a dozen times.

"Play hockey?" he now asked me.

"Just fool around," I said. "Do you?"

"Used to," he said. Then he asked, "Are you any good?"

"No," I admitted. "Even my father can skate faster than me."

"It's not how fast you go. It's what you do," the stranger said. "What's your position?"

"Used to be a forward," I said. "Now sometimes I have to play goalie."

"I was a goalie for a while."

That's when I knew he was Charlie Conacher. My father had told me about how he'd started off as a goalie, then used to carry the puck with his goalie stick until finally a coach let him play up front.

For the rest of the game I sat beside him. Every now and then he would clench his hands in frustration as the Leafs made a mistake or failed to score, and then, just before the end, he disappeared.

CHARLIE CONACHER

The whole way home my father didn't say anything, so I kept quiet until we were back in our kitchen and my mother was making us hot chocolate.

"You'll never guess who sat with us tonight," I said.

My father put the newspaper in front of his face.

"Charlie Conacher. I recognized him right away. His face was covered in scars."

"That's no way to talk about someone," my mother said. "I'm sure Charlie Conacher is a very nice man."

"He told me he used to play goal sometimes."

"I scored on him a couple of times," my father said.

That night I dreamed I was at the Gardens again. But in my dream, when the Leafs were down 3-1, Charlie Conacher stood up like a giant from the seat beside me, took a giant's step and landed on the ice wearing his old skates and his old Leaf sweater.

He looked lumpy and funny in his old uniform. His pads stuck out in crazy ways and he was still wearing the black cap he'd worn to the arena.

But as the Boston player tried to pass him, Charlie Conacher pushed him against the boards and took the puck away. Soon he was skating down the ice – not flying, but skating as fast as he could and doing something with the puck: keeping it.

Then, way over on the other side of the rink, I saw my father. He was skating, too, skating fast, skating faster than I'd ever seen him skate. He was wearing his overcoat and his hat and his scarf was flying and just as Charlie Conacher crossed the blue line, my father was sweeping in toward the goal.

I could see everything. I could see it perfectly because I was coming in behind them, slow but sure, tiny and unseen between the other players. I was cruising toward the goal with my stick out and suddenly Charlie had passed it to my father who had passed it to me and I was all alone in front of this giant goaltender but his legs were open and I poked the puck between them.

My father stopped selling tickets when my parents moved into the old age home. He could still skate and once, when I took him to the rink with my daughter, he let her beat him as she scooted up and down the boards. He watched the Saturday night games on TV, though he always said the Leafs weren't as good as they used to be. Occasionally I would take him to a game.

Before the Gardens closed he liked to stand outside with me after the game, watching the building go dark. Now I sometimes go down there alone, at night. You can almost see the ghosts coming in and out, almost hear their skates cutting up the ice, their shouts, their laughter. And then after they leave the building there's a long silence. It's something you can't hear, but you can remember.

THE FISHING
SUMMER

WHEN I WAS a boy my three uncles lived in a big wooden house by the sea. Every summer they painted it white. They had white shirts, too. On Sundays they would do the laundry and hang their white shirts out on the line, where they would flap in the wind like big raggedy gulls.

My three uncles and my mother had been children in that white wooden house. Every summer my mother would take me there for a visit.

My uncles had a fishing boat. It was like a huge rowboat with a little cabin in the middle, hardly big enough to go inside. At the end of the little cabin was the engine.

That engine had started off in a big car. Uncle Thomas, who was the oldest and had a long black beard, had taken the engine out of the car and put it in the boat. Even when it rained and stormed, Uncle Thomas could keep the motor going.

Uncle Rory was the middle uncle. His beard was black, but he kept it short by cutting it with the kitchen scissors. He could look at the sky and tell if it was safe to go out. And when the wind blew up the sea, and the clouds and fog fell over the boat like a thick soupy blanket, Uncle Rory could find the way home.

Uncle Jim was the youngest uncle and my mother's twin. He had no beard at all. He was the fisherman. He had to know where the hungry fish would be, and what they would be hungry for.

At the end of each day I would stand at the dock, waiting. The boat would come in, and my uncles would pick me up. Then we would go to the fish factory. There I would help my uncles load the fish into cardboard boxes to be weighed on the big scale. A giant with little eyes that looked like bright fox eyes would write down the numbers on a piece of paper. Then my uncles would take the paper to the cashier and get paid.

I wanted to go fishing.

"One day," Uncle Jim said, "when you get big."

"No way," my mother said. "You'll fall in and drown."

"I can swim," I said.

"You're only eight years old," my mother said.

"I started going when I was eight," said Uncle Thomas out of his big beard.

"Thomas," said my mother in a sharp voice that made the room go quiet. And I remembered another story. That my grandfather used to fish with his own brothers, and when one of the brothers got hurt, Thomas took his place. A few years later he dropped out of school and started fishing all year round. When my grandfather drowned, my other uncles started going out on the boat with Thomas.

That night I couldn't sleep. I wanted to go fishing so badly. I got dressed, then went down to the dock.

All along the bay you could hear the waves gently splish-splashing, the boats swaying and creaking against the docks. The stars were huge and bright. They hung over the sea like fruit ready to fall.

I stepped from the dock into the boat. It was strange being there alone. I wondered what it would be like to pull off the ropes, drift across the ocean and end up in some country I'd never even heard of.

The rocking of the boat made me sleepy. I went into the cabin and pulled an old blanket over myself.

I woke up to the sound of the motor hammering in my ears. I pushed back the blanket and scrambled out of the cabin. We were at sea!

But the boat was barely moving. My uncles were hauling in huge nets. Soon the boat deck was covered with narrow flopping herring twice the length of my hand, shining and silvery in the sun.

The whole time they emptied the nets into the boat, my uncles pretended I wasn't there, looking right past me, or stepping around me.

Suddenly Uncle Jim pointed at me and shouted, "Stowaway!"

The others looked as though surprised to see me. "Stowaway. Aye, Captain. Throw him overboard."

For just the tiniest little moment I wasn't sure what was going to happen. Then they all laughed and rumpled my hair and patted me on the back as though I'd done some wonderful thing.

"Your mother knows you're here and we promised not to drown you," said Uncle Rory, handing me a knife. "Now all you have to do is earn your keep."

The herring were the bait. I helped Rory cut them up while Thomas headed the boat out past the mouth of the cove. That was the farthest I'd ever been. I could still see my uncles' house, a small patchy white square against the wild heather and grass.

Soon even the cove's mouth had disappeared from view. My uncles drank tea with milk and sugar from their thermoses. They also had a thermos for me. It was filled with hot chocolate. And

in the little plastic lunch suitcase my mother had prepared for us was a bag of cookies.

"You see?" Rory said. "You did bring us good luck."

I put my hands in the sea to wash away the fishy smell. In the water my fingers looked white and dead. They came up numb with the cold, and I had to slap my hands together to warm them up.

The waves were going slip-slap against the boat. With each wave the front of the boat rose up. Then it fell down into the trough before the next wave carried it up.

"Feeling sick?"

"I'm fine," I said.

"I always used to puke," Rory said. "Then I started drinking tea. Keeps my stomach down."

"We didn't want to tell you this before you came," Thomas said, "but he might still puke any time. Better stay out of his way."

Thomas's big black beard made it hard to know when he was joking.

Suddenly in the middle of the ocean, when we could hardly see the land any more Thomas stopped the boat and threw down anchor. He baited a hook for me, and I began letting out my line.

The idea was to let it right down to the bottom of the ocean, pull it up a few feet, then jig it up and down. In those days millions of cod were parked at the bottom of the ocean, waiting for lunch. When I felt something on the line, I was supposed to wind it up.

The first couple of times I didn't have a fish at the end.

"There's currents at the bottom," Rory told me. "They feel like a fish at first. Wait for a bigger tug."

I waited. I kept getting tugs, but I didn't know if they were bigger. Finally I pulled up the line again. At the end was a huge lump. It was so big I thought it must be a rubber boot. But it turned out to be a fish.

Rory swung it into the boat. It landed with a big thump and just lay there. Thomas attached it to a stringer and put it back in the water.

Meanwhile my uncles were hauling fish up as fast as their arms could go. I kept catching them, but slower. My hands grew sore and red.

Thomas found a greasy old pair of gloves from beside the motor.

"Didn't have gloves when we were boys," he said.

"Nope," said Rory. "Dad made us stick our hands in vinegar to make them tough."

On the way back, just outside the cove, we stopped to set the herring nets again. "That way there'll be something here for us tomorrow," Rory explained.

Suddenly he whirled and threw the net out of the boat. It spread into a giant billowing mesh, then slowly settled on the water. But one of the corners got tangled up. Thomas eased about around the net, then as we came close, told me to lean over and grab the wooden float.

As I did, a little wave came up under the boat. A tiny little wave you wouldn't notice unless you'd been stupid and leaned over so far that when the wave came and the boat tipped you slid off the boat into the water.

The water was colder than ice. It filled up my shoes, put its fingers between my toes, quickly soaked my pants and started to drag them down.

I began swimming hard, kicking with all my strength, but I forgot to shout. The boat was moving away when I finally called out. My uncles turned around and saw me in the water.

Thomas cut the motor and Rory held out the paddle to me. I was too proud of my swimming to use it. I splashed right up to the boat, then reached up and grabbed the gunwale.

When I got out, I felt like my fingers had looked – white and numb. Rory grabbed the greasy blanket I'd slept under and wrapped it around me. Then he sat me on his knees and squeezed me till I got warm.

We were one of the first boats home, but my mother was down at the dock, waiting for us. I had taken off the blanket, but my soaking clothes told my mother I'd been in the water.

"How did that happen?" she demanded, glaring at my uncles.

"Now, Edith," Uncle Rory said. The same tone he'd used one Christmas when he caught her cheating at Monopoly.

"Just tell me."

"It was my fault," I said. "I was leaning over the side of the boat and I just fell in."

"Swims a lot better than you used to," Uncle Thomas said. "*He's a natural.*"

He's a natural. Uncle Thomas's voice when he called me that was the purest praise I'd ever heard. He wasn't just saying I was a good swimmer, or a good kid for taking the blame. He was saying I was part of the family. A real fisherman, like him and Rory and Jim and my grandfather's father. Right then, if he would have just asked me, just snapped his fingers, I would have jumped in the ocean and swum forever.

My mother's face turned red again. We walked up to the house. She had made a big old-fashioned tea with cookies and cakes and sandwiches to celebrate the first day fishing.

I went upstairs to change, then came down to eat. "Well," Thomas said to my mother, "aren't you going to be asking him if he enjoyed himself? Now that he's a member of the crew."

"Don't be giving me that," my mother said. "You can wait a few years. Until then he does his swimming in pools and at the beach."

"Don't be making him a baby," said Uncle Rory.

"He's a fisherman now," Jim said.

"He is not!" my mother shouted. "He *is* a baby. He's my baby and you're lucky you didn't drown him."

Uncle Thomas was standing at the counter refilling his cup. Uncle Jim just sat there, looking at my mother as though she were a stranger. Rory, too. The news was coming onto the radio with that funny little crackle it had.

I looked at my mother. She turned away from me. Now my uncles started staring at their feet, as though they'd been caught wearing girls' socks.

"I want to go," I said.

"You're not going anywhere," my mother pronounced.

The next day I was out on the boat again. My uncles were hauling up fish faster than ever. So was I, because my mother was there, helping me and supplying us all with bait.

It was a hot day, and when we got back to the cove the water felt warm on my hand. My mother put her own hand in, to test it. Rory and Thomas were standing at the front of the boat, their big tanned arms folded across their chests, satisfied with the day's work. My mother went and stood between them.

"Great day," she said.

"It was," Rory said. "To tell you the truth, Edith, I didn't know you had it in you."

"Thanks," my mother said. She had her hands on her brothers' backs. Then she gave a push. They hit the water with a giant double splash. I was the one who had to pull them in with the oars. My mother was laughing so hard, she couldn't move.

From that day we both went out with my uncles every day. By the end of the summer my arms had new muscles and my hands were tough as canvas. On the last day my uncles grabbed my mother and tossed her in. She wasn't even surprised. She just took off her boots, heaved them toward the boat, then swam to shore.

It was the last evening before we had to go back for the start of school. My uncles had caught some lobsters, and that evening we roasted them in a fire on the shore.

Then they toasted me and said how I'd become a real fisherman. Uncle Thomas gave me a drink of his coffee. It was bitter and it was raw and it was sweet. It was the taste of that summer and I never lost it.

Now the fishing factory is closed. Uncle Rory and Uncle Jim moved to the city and got married. Uncle Thomas still lives in

the old house. He runs a car repair garage that also sells newspapers and rents videos. My mother still goes to see him when she can.

After hundreds of years of everyone's grandfather and grandfather's grandfather going out to sea, no one in the village fishes any more. The fish are gone. At night you hear them talking about it on the radio and television. There are lots of words, but no fish.